Never
Follow a
DINOSAUR

Alex Latimer

PEACHTREE
ATLANTA

For Lily and Isla

Published by
PEACHTREE PUBLISHERS
1700 Chattahoochee Avenue
Atlanta, Georgia 30318-2112
www.peachtree-online.com

Text and Illustrations © 2016 by Alex Latimer

First published in Great Britain in 2016 by Picture Corgi, an imprint of Random House Children's Publishers UK
First United States version published in 2016 by Peachtree Publishers

The illustrations were created as pencil drawings, digitized, then finished with color and texture.
Printed in March 2016 in China

10 9 8 7 6 5 4 3 2 1
First Edition
ISBN 978-1-56145-704-5

Cataloging-in-Publication Data is available from the Library of Congress.

One afternoon, Joe and his sister Sally
spotted a strange set of footprints.

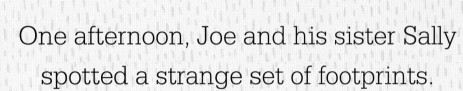

"Who do you think made those?" asked Sally.

Joe took a closer look.
"Hmmm…Given the size and shape
I think they must certainly have
been made by a dinosaur."

They followed the footprints to Willoughby's bowl. It was empty.

"It must be a very **hungry** dinosaur," said Sally. "It has eaten all of Willoughby's food!"

WILLOUGHBY

They followed the footprints
into the yard.

"Look how deep they are,"
said Joe. "It must be a very
hungry, **heavy** dinosaur to have
made such deep footprints."

They followed the footprints
right through Dad's fish pond.

"It seems to like water," said Sally.
"So it's a hungry, heavy,
swimming dinosaur!"

A little farther on, the footprints became
all squiggly and overlapping.

"What happened here?" asked Joe.

"Probably some sort of dance," said Sally.
"I'd say it's a hungry, heavy,
swimming, **dancing** dinosaur."

"What are all these leaves doing on the ground?" asked Sally.

"The dinosaur must have bumped its head on that branch," said Joe. "So it's a hungry, heavy, swimming, dancing dinosaur with a **headache**."

grumble

"And look," said Sally. "Now there
are only left foot footprints."

"He must have kicked his left foot on
this rock and hopped around in pain,"
said Joe. "So it's a hungry, heavy,
swimming, dancing dinosaur with
a headache and a **sore foot**."

grumble

And then, a little farther along,
the footprints stopped altogether.

Sally and Joe looked around for
the hungry, heavy, swimming, dancing
dinosaur with a headache and
a sore foot—but it was
nowhere to be seen.

grumble

They trudged home,
thinking of all sorts
of explanations.

But they didn't think
it had been hit by
a meteorite…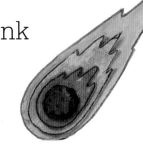

or magicked away
by a magician…

or taken by
aliens.

It was a **real mystery**.

"You should never follow a dinosaur," said Mum,
when they got home. "Especially not a **hungry** one!"

"And it probably wasn't a dinosaur at all,"
added Dad. "Because they're extinct."

But Sally and Joe were convinced it *was* a dinosaur.
And they were going to prove it.

"I know," said Sally. "Let's build a trap and catch it!"

So they spent all afternoon drawing and planning and building the perfect dinosaur trap.

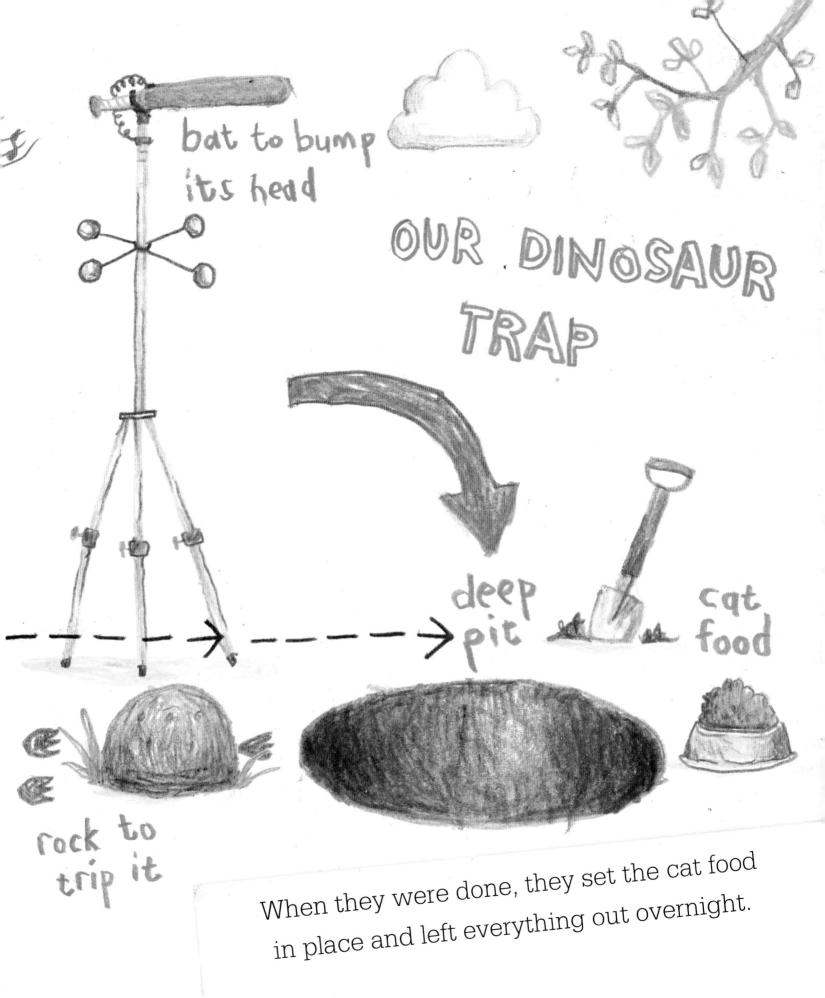

bat to bump
its head

OUR DINOSAUR
TRAP

deep
pit

cat
food

rock to
trip it

When they were done, they set the cat food
in place and left everything out overnight.

The next morning, Sally and Joe ran
out into the yard to check their trap.

The bait was gone. And there were footprints
leading right to the edge of the pit.

But
when they looked
into the hole, there was
no dinosaur.

"How did it escape?" wondered Joe.
"It's not as though it can fly."

"But what if it can?" shouted Sally.
"What if it's a **hungry, heavy,
swimming, dancing** dinosaur
with a **headache**
and a **sore foot**
and **wings**!"

Sally and Joe looked up into the sky and there,
flying above them, was the dinosaur!
It looked **very hungry** indeed.

grumble

"Uh-oh!"
said Joe.

"Run!"
yelled Sally.

grumble

But in no time the dinosaur had scooped
them up off the ground!

So you see, the reason you should never follow a
dinosaur is that some dinosaurs are just plain hungry.

However,

Luckily for Sally and Joe, once this hungry, heavy, flying dinosaur had soothed its headache, put a bandage on its sore foot, finished its dance, and had a refreshing swim—all it needed…

...was some help baking cakes!

So Sally and Joe helped the dinosaur make
(and eat) lots of delicious goodies. Yum!